KALI V. ROY

GO HEL

An Updated Guide to

JESSE RIGGLE

TOOLS

Dante's Underworld

P.

For Eva, my demon-heart's twin.
Thanks to Evan, Ryan, Laughlin, and Garrick for giving me hells.

AN IMPRINT OF ZEST BOOKS

Connect with Zest! ————————————

- zestbooks.net/blog   - facebook.com/zestbook
- zestbooks.net/contests   - facebook.com/BooksWithATwist
- twitter.com/zestbooks   - pinterest.com/zestbooks

35 Stillman Street, Suite 121, San Francisco, CA 94107 / www.zestbooks.net

Text copyright © 2015 by Onnesha Roychoudhuri
Illustrations copyright © 2015 by Jesse Riggle

Design by Adam Grano

Humor / General
Library of Congress data available
ISBN: 978-1-936976-82-9

Manufactured in the U.S.A.
DOC 10 9 8 7 6 5 4 3 2 1
4500520524

Dear Reader,

If you have nothing but fond feelings for your fellow man—even the one who stands ahead of you in line with absolutely no clear sense of whether he wants the muffin or the croissant—then put this book down. It's not for you.

What you hold in your hands is the definitive guide to the underworld. Not since the 1300s, when Dante accidentally stumbled below, has anyone explored that infamous pit of perdition. Lucky for you, I've recently been to hell, and I bring good news: Since Dante's time, the Beelzebub business has been booming. With dozens of new circles of hell (because, let's be honest, nine just wasn't cutting it), cranks of the world can finally rejoice. Chances are there's a special circle for everyone irksome in your life.

The devil is always in the details, which is why this book is a vital addition to any proper curmudgeon's library. I offer you this arsenal of damnation in the hope that, from now on, when you tell someone to go to hell, you can be as specific as possible.

So now, dear reader, join me if you dare, on a spectacular and horrible tour through hells.

—Kali V. Roy

Abandon all hope

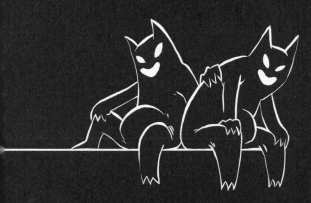

ye who enter here.

Entitled Roommates

You ate all our soup.
You never bought soap.

You acted as though you were king.

Now, tuck right in—
you'll eat the chef's special:

A bisque made from fresh Irish Spring.

Ghastly Chewers

You chomped and you gnashed
through all of life's meals

Without ever once closing your jaw.

Here there's no need
for a fork or a knife—

You'll sip all of your
meals through a straw.

Cell Phone Soliloquizers

"It's cloudy outside."
"I'm drunk at a bar."

Your narration just drove us insane.

———◆◇◆———

But now it's your turn to silently stew

As Fran Drescher gives you a migraine.

PDA-ers

On trains and at bars,
the two of you smooched

While we tried to keep down our lunch.

———————◆◇◆———————

Here on this island,
you'll have all you need:

Each other—and freedom to munch.

———————◆◇◆———————

Chronic
Name-Forgetters

"Oh, hi."
"I'm sorry, have we met before?"

Your poor memory should
have caused shame.

◆◆◆

Here at this party,
you'll shake many hands

But you just can't remember your name.

Puritanical Dining-Mates

"No time for dessert. My jog is at six!"

Superior lifestyle: noted.

—◆◇◆—

Now—just relax!—while you're
stuffed with sweet treats

And force-fed 'til utterly bloated.

Close-Talkers

Each step back just made you come closer.

Your nearness! It caused sheer psychosis.

Here's your new twin,
conjoined at the chest:

She's chatty and has halitosis.

Over-the-Shoulder Readers

We never could finish our paperbacks.

It's your eyeballs that we have to thank.

Enjoy this collection, made just for you

Filled with books that
have pages—all blank.

Selfish Bedmates

You slept like a nighttime Napoleon,

Conquering every inch of the bed.

Now tuck yourself in;
This cot's all for you.

(Mind the tiny sharp spikes made of lead.)

Movie Chatterboxes

Cinema blatherers vexed us with chat

And kept us from joining the dots.

This hellish venue's come up with a fix:

Your seatmates here spoil all plots.

Impossible Packaging Designers

We tried scissors and knives
—even our teeth—

But nothing could do enough damage.

◇◆◇

Leaving this circle's a cinch:
Take this pill!

It's sealed, but I'm sure you can manage.

Cable Company Executives

You can't give us back the hours we spent

Disputing those charges unholy.

———◆◇◆———

Now hold the line forever and ever

While listening to Kenny G solely.

Cell Phone Designers

Our phones were designed
to die a quick death

In what you called
"planned obsolescence."

—◇◈◇—

Enjoy being reborn again and again

Without making it past adolescence.

DAY 1   ...   DAY 666

Train-Stormers

Selfish commuters in hours of rush

Pushed in before we could get out.

How greedy, how rude!
Now here's your new job:

Swim upstream against legions of trout.

Seat Hogs

You spread your legs wide
and took up two spots;

We were squashed like a parcel of meat.

———◆◇◆———

Here you'll find plenty
of like-minded friends

Competing for only one seat.

Inventor of the Saucer

These dishes were made
to catch all our spills,

But really just caused them instead.

Down here their vile creator will take

His hot sugared tea on the head.

Malcolm Gladwell

It's counterintuitive, therefore it's true!

Your pop science made *real* experts cry.

———◆◇◆———

Now you've got time to test a new theory:

Improved vision by poking your eyes.

State-ers of the Obvious

"Eat that whole pie,
and you may feel quite sick."

"Want cocktails?
They're served at the bar."

Welcome to hell,
you'll just love it down here:

You'll never not know where you are.

Social Media Hermits

While you "liked" every
photo on Facebook,

A "hello" in real life was too much.

Now you're surrounded
by super-hot dates.

You can ogle but never can touch.

Re-Gifters

That sweater looked awfully familiar—

'Cause I gave you the same thing last fall.

Now is your chance to find a new gift:

It's forever Yule time at this mall.

Wait-Staff Abusers

"Hey, you" was your name for all servers

When complaining the food wasn't hot.

This diner (no stars) serves only one meal:

Scalding borscht with rat,
right from the pot.

Cheapskates

We all split the check,
but still came up short.

Your stinginess gave us frustration.

You didn't include the tax or the tip,

So now you'll serve sans compensation.

Indecisive Order-ers

You brought deli lines to a standstill

Debating: the chips... or a peach?

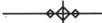

Here's what you get for making us wait:

Tasty treats!—all juuust out of reach.

Boastful Grumps

"Missing your girlfriend?
Mine cheated on me."

Being the saddest of all was your biz.

Now you'll compete
with a special new group:

Try one-upping the cast of *Les Mis*.

Joke-Nabbers

Your punch lines were filched!
You stole all our jokes!

Letting strangers think you were a card.

So now you'll perform
your new stand-up set

To an audience of the Queen's Guard.

Internet Trolls

Thank you for taking the time to suggest

That our brains were
far smaller than peas.

Now you'll deliver your comments direct

To real trolls who are angry as bees.

Public Groomers

What horror, to watch you go at it,

And flick your half-moons on our laps!

But now it's your turn to start dodging.

(These chimps do love
throwing their craps.)

Dream Recount-ers

You held us captive to tell us about

How you dreamt you invented red wine.

———◆◇◆———

Now it's your turn to listen to drivel:

Ayn Rand's books!—
and they're read by Ben Stein.

Potluck Cheats

Betty baked brownies;
Tom brought the beers;

And you brought your specialty: squat.

———◈———

Here is your chance to finally share.

Your hell-mate likes liver (a lot).

ATM Lurkers

We didn't much like your
breath on our necks

(Worse than fees when
withdrawing some dough).

This guy right here shares
your weird sense of space,

And comes with you when you have to go.

Shoddy Washers

You said they were clean!
Those plates always had

Fish scales and rice bits that still clung.

Now you're in charge of this dirty pig-pen.

Your scouring tool? It's your tongue.

Chronically Late Arrivers

Minutes ticked by and
the food grew quite cold.

You never showed when you were due.

———◆———

Down here the clock
never changes at all—

At last: Time has lost track of you.

Unnecessarily Firm Hand-Shakers

No, it wasn't a pleasure to meet you!

Our fingers lost all their good feeling.

I wish you good luck on kitchen prep here.

Boneless hands have trouble with peeling.

Reply All-ers

All forty-five people had to hear why

You missed young Jack's
wedding down South.

Prefer to skip hell? Just say so right now.

(But—oops!—seems you've
misplaced your mouth.)

Baby Puppeteers

"Mommy is being so stubborn," you cried,

As you waved the poor baby's fat arms.

Now when the devil gets bored—
you're his man!

You'll fit on his fist like a charm.

Loud Typers

Office percussionists jangled our brains

With the clack of their
QWERTY-filled songs.

So now—what a band!—
they're fitted with pots

And rung every minute like gongs.

Strangers Who Tell You to Smile

"Aw, come on, sweetheart,
it can't be that bad!"

"Go on: Turn that frown upside-down!"

Down here you'll relive
your own darkest times

With a grin that is fit for a clown.

Phone Fixators

While we tried to
explain how our dog died,

You checked email and then sent a text.

It's just you and your phone—solo at last.

Only problem is: You're a T-rex.

Sipping their whiskeys while doling out fates,
This punishment comes a bit tardy.

Our hells-creators, two real misanthropes,
Must now host a perpetual party.

———◆———

KALI V. ROY, *author*
JESSE RIGGLE, *illustrator*